With thanks to our family for their support and encouragement, and to Phil for walking us through to our finish.

Because all children should have the same opportunity to pursue their dreams and passions, a portion of all proceeds will be donated to Children of Promise NYC.

Contributor credits:
Artist: Azure Bush
Editor: Philip Luchon

LiLi Rabbit, Eat Your Vegetables!

Written by: Nahndi Bush

Illustrated by: Azure Bush

This is LiLi.

LiLi is a very happy rabbit.

She is playful, curious, and a little stubborn.

She likes being scratched behind her ears,

and she loves her girl.

She plays with her rabbit toys, and chews on her wood sticks.

LiLi loves to eat! She could eat grapes,
strawberries, apples, and blueberries every
day.

But what LiLi DIDN'T like was when her girl would say, "You need to eat your vegetables, LiLi. They're good for you!" LiLi did NOT like vegetables.

Vegetables would sit in LiLi's bowl for days.

They would get moldy and stinky, and she would not touch them.

No matter how hard her girl would try, LiLi refused to eat her vegetables.

What LiLi loves most of all, are WABBIT TREATS!!!

LiLi could eat WABBIT TREATS every day, all day, for breakfast, lunch, and dinner.

But she was not allowed. "Wabbit treats are not good for you to eat all day," her girl would say. "Just now and then as a special treat". LiLi did not like that.

One day LiLi was playing in her favorite closet, pulling clothes onto the floor to make a comfy rabbit bed.

The closet was nice and messy now, the way she liked it!

LiLi pulled the soft, fluffy sleeve of a sweatshirt from one of the shelves.

Suddenly,

Sniff
Sniff

WABBIT TREATS!

LiLi pounced into the pile and began eating. CRUNCH! She ate 3. CHOMP! She ate 5 more.

MUNCH, MUNCH, MUNCH! LiLi kept eating until the WHOLE pile was gone!

Then LiLi snuggled down on the soft black sweatshirt and made a nice bed for herself.

After a little while, LiLi did not feel so well.

LiLi's stomach growled, and bubbled, and rumbled.

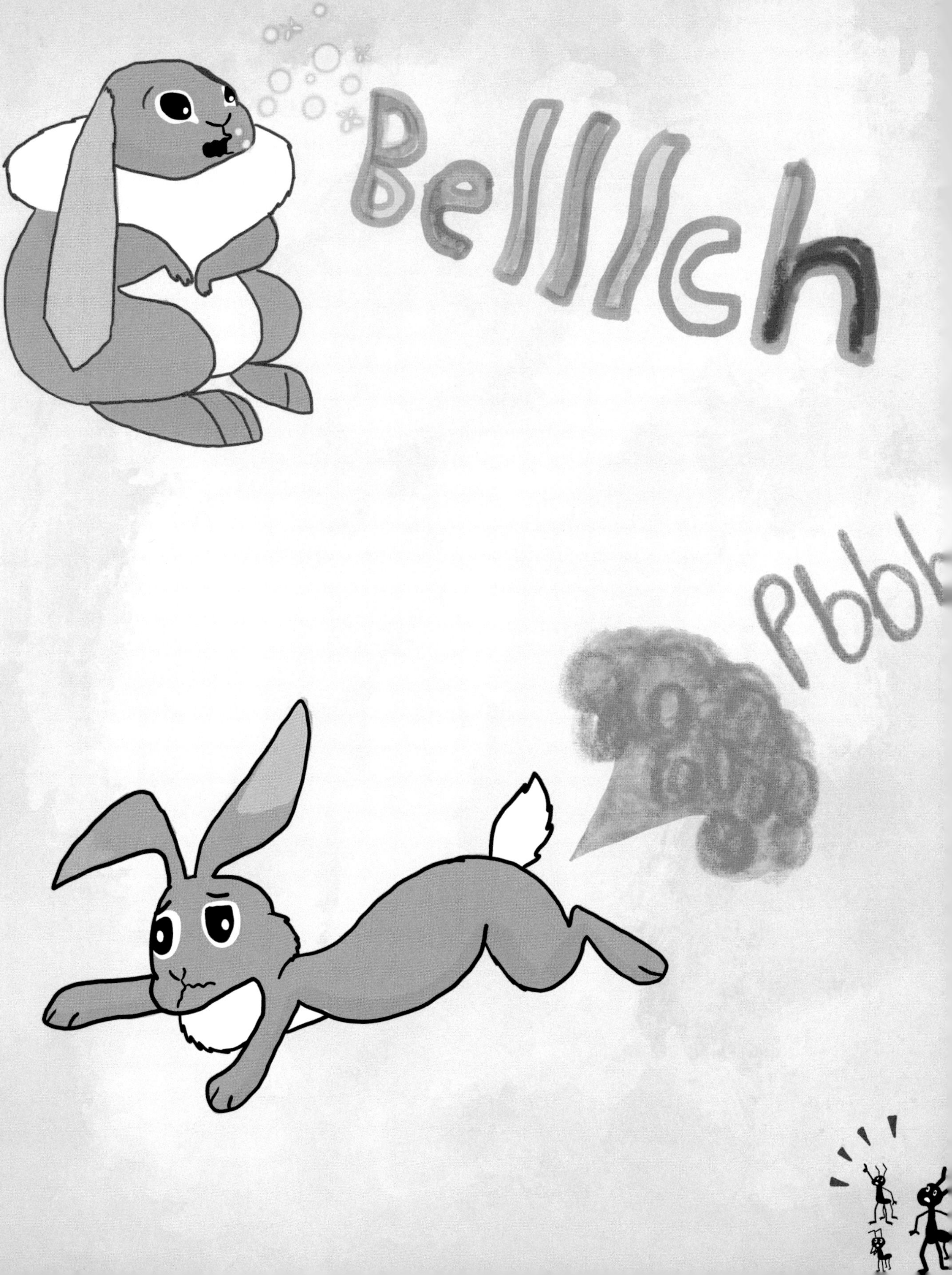
Belllch
Pbb

LiLi was miserable.

All she could do was lay there on the closet floor moaning, and wishing she had never touched a Wabbit Treat.

That night, LiLi's girl opened the closet and found LiLi lying there. "Ohhhh, Lili, what did you do?"

She saw the empty bag next to LiLi and knew.

She picked LiLi up and took her to bed. She cuddled with LiLi until they fell asleep.

It was a long night.

The next morning, LiLi felt better.

"LiLi," her girl said, "you can't ever do that again. No more Wabbit Treats for a month! You must start eating vegetables like other rabbits."

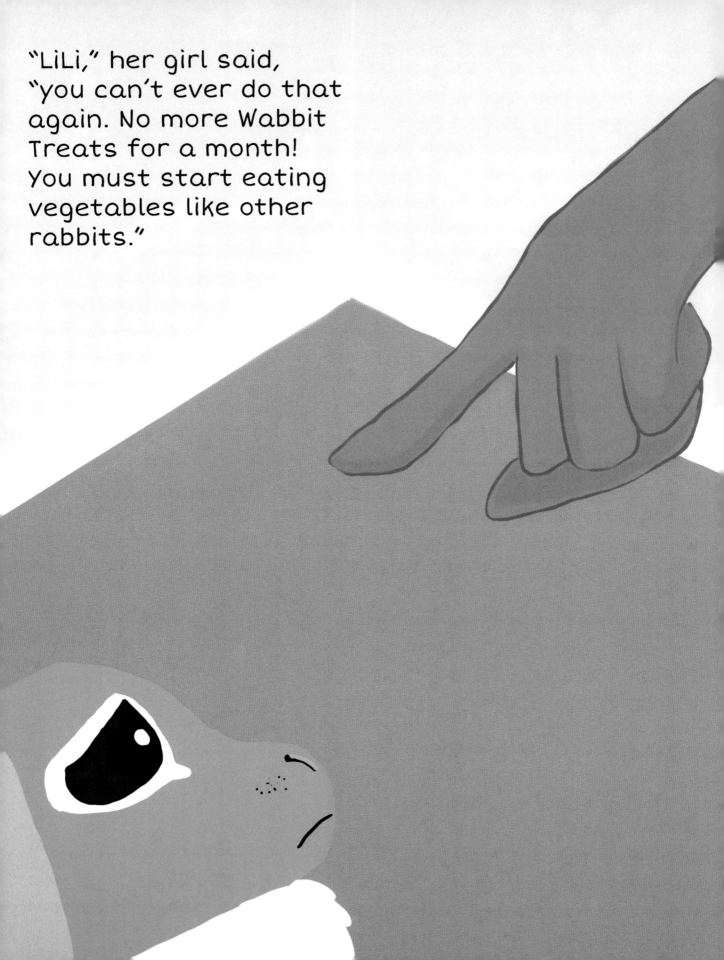

When LiLi hopped over to her bowl the next morning, she saw a pile of green stuff. She turned her back.

"Hmmph!"

LiLi was SO hungry!

Finally, LiLi was desperate. She scooched over to her bowl and sniffed a leaf.

Then she licked it.

Then she nibbled.

Heyyyyyyyy! This was crispy and juicy! LiLi crunched a radish, munched a stalk of broccoli, and chomped on a crunchy carrot. Before she knew it, the bowl was empty.

Every day, LiLi's girl would fill her bowl with fresh vegetables, and LiLi made them disappear.

LiLi's fur became thicker and glossier. She was faster, and could jump higher than ever before.

Yes, LiLi LOVED eating her vegetables now.

But she still loved
her Wabbit treats!

Azure Bush is a high school student from New Jersey who aspires to be an illustrator and animator for Disney Studios, and work with animals. LiLi Rabbit came into her life in February 2020, just before the COVID-19 pandemic and lockdown ensued. This book grew out of a desire to turn a difficult year into an opportunity to bring joy to others.

Nahndi Bush is a mom to Azure and her two brothers, Loring and Logan, and wife to Loring Sr. She is a practicing physician who enjoys writing, and treasured the opportunity to bond creatively with her teenage daughter for this project.

Made in the USA
Columbia, SC
02 May 2021